Mars

Tim Goss

Heinemann Library
Chicago, Illinois

Customer Service 888-454-2279

Visit our website at www.heinemannlibrary.com

Layout by Roslyn Broder
Illustrations by Calvin J. Hamilton
Printed in Hong Kong

07 06 05 04 03
10 9 8 7 6 5 4 3 2 1

Library of Congress Cataloging-in-Publication Data
Goss, Tim, 1958-

  Mars / by Tim Goss.
     v. cm. -- (The universe)
Includes bibliographical references and index.
Contents: Where in the sky is Mars? -- Why does Mars look red? -- How is
Mars different from Earth? -- What would I see if I went to Mars? --
What's in the middle of Mars? -- Is there life on Mars? -- Could I ever
go to Mars?
  ISBN 1-58810-912-7 (HC), 1-4034-0613-8 (Pbk)
  1. Mars (Planet)--Juvenile literature. [1. Mars (Planet)] I. Title.
II. Series.
  QB641 .G68 2002
  523.43--dc21
                              2002000814

Acknowledgments
The author and publisher are grateful to the following for permission to reproduce copyright
material: pp. 4, 5, 6, 9B, 16, 19, 24, 25, 26, 27, 28 NASA/JPL/Caltech; p. 7 NASA and the Hubble
Heritage Team (STScI/AURA); p. 8 PIRL/University of Arizona/NASA; p. 9T NASA, James Bell/Cornell
University, Michael Wolff/Space Science Institute, and the Hubble Heritage Team (STScI/AURA); p. 10
Lowell Georgia/Corbis; p. 11 NASA/Space Telescope Science Institute; p. 12 NASA/U.S. Geological
Survey; pp. 13B, 21 NASA/Ames Research Center; pp. 14, 15, 17, 20, 29 NASA/JPL/Malin Space
Science Systems; p. 18 Steve Lee/University of Colorado, James Bell/Cornell University, Michael
Wolff/Space Science Institute, and NASA; p. 19 Courtesy of Calvin J. Hamilton/www.solarviews.com;
p. 21T Bettmann/Corbis; pp. 22, 23 NASA/Kennedy Space Center

Cover photograph by Steve Lee/University of Colorado, James Bell/Cornell University, Michael
Wolff/Space Science Institute, and NASA

The publisher would like to thank Geza Gyuk and Diana Challis of the Adler Planetarium for their
comments in the preparation of this book.

Some words are shown in bold, **like this.** You can find out what
they mean by looking in the glossary.

Contents

Where in the Sky Is Mars?

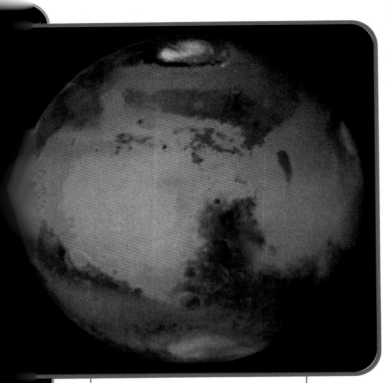

*This photo of Mars was taken by the Hubble Space **Telescope** in 1997.*

If you look in the early night sky just above the horizon, you can sometimes see a tiny, red **planet** glowing far away. This is the planet Mars. The best time of day to see it depends on the time of year.

Mars is one of the nine planets in our **solar system.** It is one of the four planets in our solar system known as the Rocky Planets. The other three are Mercury, Venus, and Earth. Mars is the farthest Rocky Planet from the Sun.

Why is it called Mars?

When people looked at Mars long ago, its red color made them think of blood and wars. They thought that the planet was like a strong soldier who was always ready for battle. For that reason, the ancient Romans named the red planet after Mars, their god of war.

The solar system

The solar system is made of all the planets, **comets,** and **asteroids** that circle the Sun. The Sun's **gravity** pulls on all of the objects in our solar system. If it were not for the pull of the Sun, the planets would travel in straight lines. This would send them out into deep space! The force of gravity keeps the planets in regular paths around the Sun called **orbits.**

Mars is the fourth planet from the top, going along the curve. Pluto is missing from this collection of images because no spacecraft has traveled to Pluto yet to take any pictures.

Mars is Earth's neighbor

Mars is the fourth planet from the Sun. Its neighbors are Earth and Jupiter. Between Mars and Jupiter is a large belt, or grouping, of asteroids. Sometimes Mars and Earth are close together as they orbit the Sun. This happens about every two years and two months. Mars is opposite the Sun in the sky at this time, so it is said to be in **opposition.** Mars comes closest to Earth about every fifteen to seventeen years.

The time it takes a planet to rotate one time around its **axis** is called a **day.** Like Earth, Mars needs about 24 hours to rotate one time. The time it takes for a planet to orbit the Sun is called a **year.** It takes Mars about 687 Earth days to orbit the Sun. This means that a year on Mars lasts almost two Earth years.

Why Does Mars Look Red?

Mars is often called the Red **Planet** because it shines with a red-orange light in the sky. People from ancient times up to only a few years ago used to wonder why Mars was red. In the 1960s and 1970s, the National Aeronautics and Space Administration (NASA) sent **space probes** to Mars. One of the things they found out while exploring the planet was why Mars is red.

This was the first color picture taken of the surface of Mars. You can see how red the soil is.

There is rust in the soil

Over millions of years, water and oxygen in the **atmosphere** of Mars soaked into the rocks and started **chemical reactions** with the rocks and dust. This could have happened because Martian rocks and dust have a lot of iron in them. Iron is a metal. When a rock with iron in it mixes with water and oxygen, the chemical reactions make rust. Over time, almost all of the oxygen in Mars's atmosphere was soaked up by the rocks of Mars to make rust. Now there is so much rust staining the rocks and dust of Mars that the entire planet looks red.

How Is Mars Different from Earth?

Mars is about half the size of Earth and much colder. There is no rain to water plants or air for animals to breathe, so there is no life on Mars. There are no oceans on Mars or dirt that would be the right kind for growing plants. Mars has lots of rocks and no trees. Seasons last twice as long because a **year** on Mars is twice as long as Earth's. There is not enough oxygen in the air on Mars for humans to breathe.

Mars is colder than Earth

Mars and all of the planets in our **solar system orbit** around the Sun. The Sun supplies almost all of the heat energy to the planets. The farther a planet gets from the Sun, the colder it gets. Mars is much farther away from the Sun than Earth, so Mars receives less heat.

Mars also loses heat easily because it has a very thin atmosphere compared to the Earth. An atmosphere works sort of like a blanket. Earth has a thick atmosphere that keeps it warm, while Mars's thin atmosphere lets the heat out quickly. During the winter months, temperatures on Mars can be as low as −189°F (−123°C). This is 60 degrees colder than the coldest temperature recorded on Earth. During the summer months, temperatures on Mars can climb as high as 63°F (17°C). This would feel like a spring day on Earth.

This picture of Mars shows some of its frosty, white water-ice clouds.

You could not breathe on Mars

Our **atmosphere** on Earth has many gases. It contains a very important gas called oxygen. We need oxygen to breathe. The atmosphere of Mars does not have enough oxygen gas for humans to breathe. Astronauts would need special space suits with oxygen tanks to explore the **planet.**

When Mars first formed, gases were trapped inside the planet's atmosphere. Over millions of years, many of these gases slowly escaped into outer space. Much of the oxygen that was in the atmosphere is now in the form of rust or frozen water. There are no plants or other life forms on Mars to produce more oxygen. The atmosphere of Mars now is mostly made up of carbon dioxide gas. This is the gas that humans breathe out. The air on Mars is so thin, it would be impossible for us to breathe there.

Clouds on Mars are made of water ice and reddish dust particles. Dust storms on Mars have been known to stretch across the whole planet and last for months.

Mars has bad weather

Space probes to Mars have taught us that Mars has thin clouds, high winds, and huge dust storms. These dust storms can be 5 miles (8 kilometers) high.

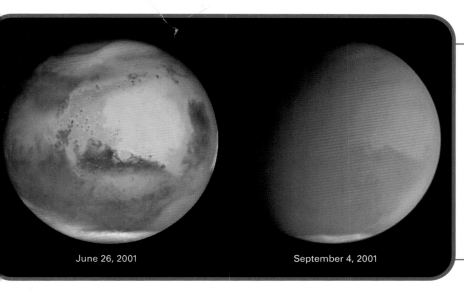

June 26, 2001

September 4, 2001

The image on the right shows how completely a dust storm once covered Mars. The details of the planet that we can see in the image on the left are completely hidden by the storm.

During a **day** on Mars, the temperatures change a lot. The average daytime temperature on Mars during the summer is −10°F (−23°C). The temperature at Vanda Station in Antarctica on Earth gets up to 59°F (15°C). That is much warmer than an average day on Mars. The average nighttime temperature on Mars during the summer is −135°F (−57°C). Temperatures on Mars change more during just one day than temperatures on Earth change during whole seasons!

A photo of the surface of Mars shows that there is a thin coating of ice on the rocks and soil.

What Would I See if I Went to Mars?

If you stood at the north or south pole of Mars, you would see lots and lots of ice. The north half of the **planet** also has flat desert areas. The south part of the planet has deep canyons. Across the planet, there are also tall cliffs, huge **volcanoes,** dried-up riverbeds, and huge holes in the ground called **craters.**

It always looks like winter at the poles

Imagine placing a giant belt around the middle of a planet so that the top and bottom parts are equal. The top half is called the planet's northern **hemisphere** and the bottom half is called the southern hemisphere. The imaginary "belt" on the planet is called the **equator.**

The Viking *lander and its* rover *collected samples of the soil on Mars for scientists to study.*

The area at the top of the northern hemisphere is called the north pole. The area at the bottom part of the southern hemisphere is called the south pole. Each of these places on Mars has long seasons of very little sunlight. During those winter seasons, gases in these areas get very cold and freeze into a type of ice. Each hemisphere on Mars, like Earth, has a polar cap. This is a huge piece of ice that covers part of the planet's surface. Just like on Earth, the ice caps on Mars grow each **day** during

Are Mars's ice caps different than Earth's?

Mars has two ice caps—one at its northern tip and one at the southern tip. Scientists think that the ice caps are mostly made of frozen carbon dioxide gas. This is the gas that humans breathe out. Carbon dioxide ice is much colder than the water ice that makes up Earth's ice caps. Scientists have also found some frozen water ice in Mars's northern ice cap.

the winter as more and more ice forms. However, on Mars, this ice is frozen gas rather than frozen water.

Summer on Mars

Suppose you place a tray of ice outside in the sunlight. If the outside temperature is warm enough, the ice will quickly disappear. This is because the heat energy from the Sun's light rays melts the ice. Something like this happens on Mars. As a Martian polar cap gets more light during the summer, the heat energy raises the temperature. The ice caps shrink as their edges boil away in the form of carbon dioxide gas.

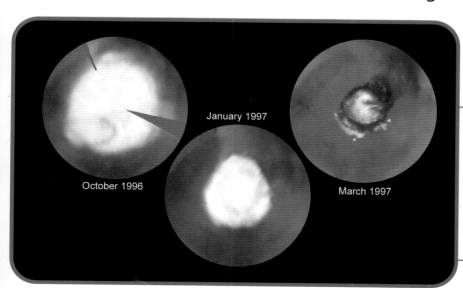

October 1996

January 1997

March 1997

Scientists have studied how the size of Mars's northern polar cap changes over time.

Canyons and craters

The canyons of Mars are long, deep cuts in the surface that stretch for many miles. The largest group of canyons on Mars is called the Valles Marineris, or Mariner Valley. It was named after the spacecraft that first photographed it—*Mariner 9*. The canyons are about 6 miles (9.7 kilometers) deep and 400 miles (644 kilometers) across. It takes more than six hours to travel 400 miles in a car on a highway.

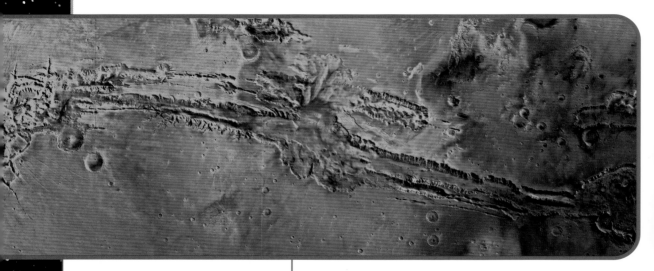

Mariner Valley is the length of the entire United States. If the separate canyons were placed end to end, they would stretch much further.

On some parts of Mars you can find groups of large **craters.** Scientists believe that long ago the surface was hit by a series of huge rocks from outer space called **meteors.** Rocks that crash into a **planet's** surface are called **meteorites.** When huge meteorites crashed into Mars, they exploded, making craters in the surface of the planet. These large meteorite impacts, or crashes, can create a stronger explosion than any nuclear explosion.

This Martian meteorite was found on Earth in 1996.

What has come to Earth from Mars?

Scientists who study Mars have been very lucky. Small rocks from Mars have actually fallen from the sky and landed on Earth. These rocks are called meteorites. They were blasted from the surface of Mars by a huge meteorite impact, or crash. These rocks got thrown off the planet and into space at speeds of more than 1 mile (1.6 kilometers) per second.

Most meteorites from Mars have been found in the Antarctic. Swiss scientists found the eighteenth Martian meteorite identified on Earth in the Oman Desert in 2001. It is gray and about the size of a fist. Fluids deep inside it might hold bubbles of trapped gases from the **atmosphere** on Mars. Scientists hope to learn more about the surface and atmosphere of the Red Planet by studying this meteorite.

Mars has volcanoes

When Mars first formed, the inside of the **planet** was very hot. High temperatures inside Mars caused the rocks to melt and form **magma.** Massive streams of magma flowed upward toward the surface. The melted rock exploded onto the surface of Mars.

When magma reaches the surface of a planet, it is called **lava.** Long ago, lava on Mars poured out and spread across the planet's surface. As it slowly cooled, the lava changed back to solid rock. Huge mountains of cooled lava, called **volcanoes,** formed on the surface.

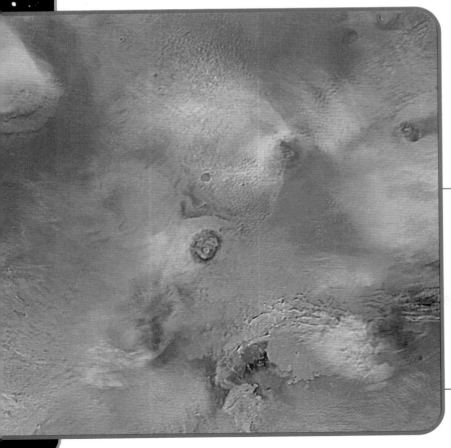

*Most of the volcanoes on Mars are found in a part of the northern **hemisphere** called the Tharsis Region. The region stretches about 5,000 miles (8,000 kilometers).*

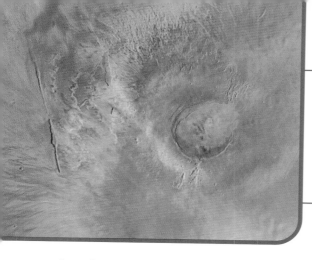

Mount Arsia, shown here, is one of the largest known volcanoes. Only Mount Olympus is larger.

The four largest volcanoes on Mars are named Mount Olympus, Mount Arsia, Mount Pavonis, and Mount Ascraeus. There is no sign that any of the volcanoes will erupt again, but scientists are not certain.

Mount Olympus is the tallest volcano of any planet in our **solar system.** It is more than 15 miles (25 kilometers) high and 435 miles (700 kilometers) wide. It is three times as tall as Mount Everest, the tallest mountain on Earth. It is also wider than the country of England. Scientists think that Mount Olympus last erupted about 200 million years ago.

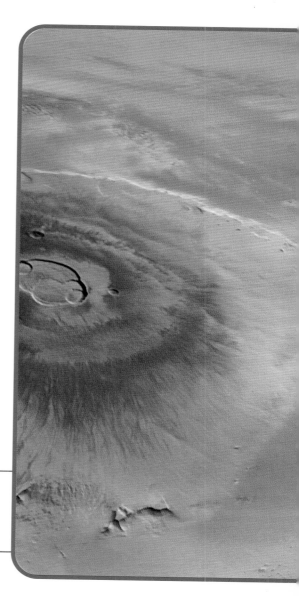

This photo shows what Mount Olympus looks like from about 560 miles (900 kilometers) above the surface of Mars.

Looking up at the moons of Mars

If you were on Mars, you would have to be near its **equator** to see its two **moons.** Each Martian moon is a lump of rock only a few miles across. The moons **orbit** Mars much more closely than our Moon orbits Earth. If you went too far toward the north or south pole, though, you would not see the moons. This is because Mars's moons orbit the **planet** near the equator.

In this collection of images, an asteroid (top) is compared to the moons of Mars. Deimos is at the lower left corner, while Phobos is at the lower right corner.

An **astronomer** named Asaph Hall discovered the moons in August 1877. He was using a **telescope** at the U.S. Naval Observatory in Washington, D.C. The moons looked like tiny specks of light. Hall could tell they were moons because they were slowly orbiting the planet.

The moon closest to Mars is called Phobos. It is also the larger of the two moons. It orbits quickly, circling Mars about every eight hours. Scientists predict that Phobos will crash into Mars in only a few tens of millions of years. That is a short period of time in the history of the universe.

What do their names mean?

The Greeks named the planet Mars *Ares* after their god of battle. Asaph Hall named the planet's two moons after two sons of Ares. *Phobos* means "fear," and *Deimos* means "panic."

The other moon that orbits Mars is called Deimos. It is more than twice as far away from Mars as Phobos. Deimos completes an orbit of Mars about every 31 hours. A spacecraft orbited Deimos from a short distance to photograph it. The photos of Deimos show that the moon is coated in dust.

Both moons are potato-shaped rather than round. We know about their shape because of photos taken by spacecraft sent to Mars. Scientists believe that these two moons were once **asteroids.** They were probably pulled into Mars's orbit by the force of the planet's **gravity.** Both moons have many **craters** from being struck by **meteorites.** Scientists believe the moons may be as old as Mars itself.

This is a photograph of Mars's moon Phobos.

What Is Inside Mars?

Beneath the surface of each Rocky **Planet** are layers called the **crust,** the **mantle,** and the **core. Space probes** that we have sent to Mars have taught us a lot about what the inside of Mars is made of. But we still need to learn a lot more about our neighbor planet.

Future space probes will probably help us understand more about the inside of Mars.

*This image of Mars focuses on the Tharsis Region, where the planet's largest **volcanoes** are found.*

The core

The center of a planet is called the core. Scientists think that the core of Mars is made up of iron, just like Earth's core. They are not yet sure what it is made of. Scientists have not yet been able to estimate the temperature of the core of Mars. They also cannot be sure of the exact size of the core. They do know that Mars's core is very hot and is probably solid.

Imagine you were traveling from the center of Mars to the surface. You would travel about 1,000 miles (1,609 kilometers) through a sea of **magma** before finally leaving the core. One thousand miles is a long way!

If you were in a car on a highway, it would take you more than fifteen hours to travel that far.

The mantle

The next part of the interior of Mars is called the mantle. It is shaped like a thick ball that covers the core. It is made mostly of solid rock, but it can bend like plastic. The rock in the mantle can bend because the temperatures are very high. To pass through the mantle, you would have to travel almost 1,000 miles (1,609 kilometers).

The crust

The last part of your trip would be very short. The outside layer of Mars is called the crust. The crust of a planet acts like an eggshell. It is thin compared to the core and the mantle. It is also hard and it covers everything inside. The crust of Mars sits on top of the mantle and is made of solid rock. The rust-red rocks of Mars make up the outside part of the crust, called the surface.

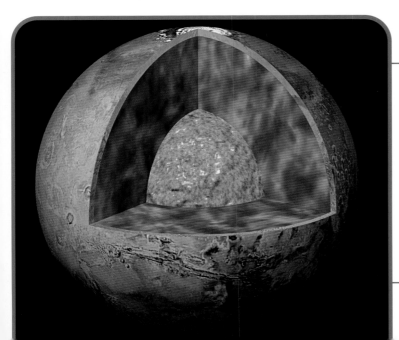

Scientists estimate where each layer of a planet begins and ends. This helps them learn more about the planet. This illustration shows where Mars's layers might begin and end.

Is There Life on Mars?

Scientists have determined that there is no life on Mars. The conditions there would not support life. There is no water and no oxygen. There is also radiation at levels that would kill any living thing on the **planet.**

Even the largest canyons on Mars would have been too small for Schiaparelli to see with his telescope.

People used to think there was life on Mars

More than 100 years ago, an Italian **astronomer** named Giovanni Schiaparelli studied Mars with his new **telescope.** Schiaparelli saw many lines crisscrossing the planet. He drew sketches of the lines and showed them to friends. He called these lines *canali,* which is the Italian word for channels. Some people who read reports about the lines on Mars began to think that Mars really had canals. They thought that very smart creatures must have built the canals. Maybe there was alien life on Mars!

For almost 100 years, people still believed there were "canals" on Mars. But in the 1960s, NASA scientists sent a **space probe** that took pictures of Mars. In the 1970s, they sent two space probes that actually landed on Mars. They found no signs of life on the planet. There were no canals across its surface.

Were aliens attacking Earth?

In 1938, an actor and writer named Orson Welles scared many Americans. He was the host of a radio show in which actors read plays. On Halloween night, Welles and other actors presented a play based on a novel by H.G. Wells called *War of the Worlds.* The novel was about an attack on Earth by aliens from Mars. The show began with what sounded like a real news flash about an attack on Earth. It sounded so real that many Americans really thought it was happening. They were terrified. They thought Martians were taking over Earth!

There may have been life on Mars in the past

There is not any water on Mars now, but there used to be. Photos of the planet show grooves, or channels, in the surface that must have been made by rivers. Mars must have once had a different type of **atmosphere** and different surface conditions to allow for surface water. After studying Martian **meteorites,** some scientists have suggested that there may have been bacteria on Mars billions of years ago. Many scientists disagree, however. No one knows for certain.

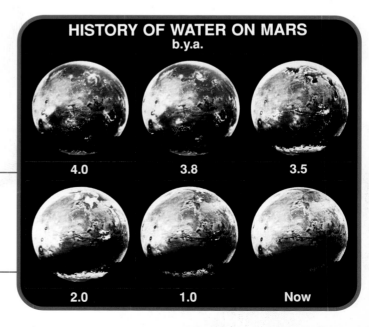

HISTORY OF WATER ON MARS
b.y.a.

| 4.0 | 3.8 | 3.5 |
| 2.0 | 1.0 | Now |

This is a scientist's idea of the history of water on Mars from 4 billion years ago (b.y.a.) to the present time.

Could I Ever Go to Mars?

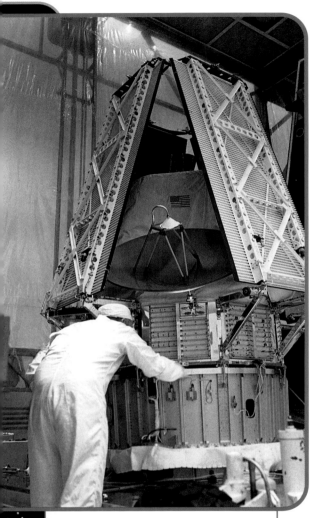

This photo was taken while workers were running final checks on the Mariner 9 *space probe before its launch.*

Have you ever wondered if you could take a trip to Mars? Maybe someday people will be able to catch rides with missions to outer space. On some missions, spaceships just fly by a **planet.** On other missions, the spaceships land. These spaceships do not always have room for people, though, so you would have to plan your trip carefully.

Packing for your trip

If you did go to Mars, you would need a lot of help for your trip. Remember that the weather on Mars can be very cold. You would need a special space suit and an air tank for breathing. Removing your space suit for even a couple of seconds would be deadly! You would also need a spaceship to get you there. Even in a very fast rocket, it would take at least six months or a year to get there. You might also want to bring a small truck called a land **rover** for traveling across the rocky surface. It would be tough hiking around all those rocks, canyons, and **volcanoes.**

The *Mariner* missions

Since the early 1960s, NASA has been sending **space probes** to study Mars. The first U.S. space probes to Mars were called the *Mariner* missions. In 1964, NASA sent *Mariner 4* to travel past the Red Planet. It took seven months to travel to Mars. It brought a television camera, a **telescope,** and other instruments to study the planet.

Mariner 4 flew past Mars from a very far distance, but its cameras took 22 photographs of the Red Planet. The photos showed us that the surface of Mars has many rust-colored rocks, **craters,** and lots of dust. But there were no canals or other signs of life on the planet. People were disappointed to see that the planet looked more like Earth's Moon than Earth. In 1969, NASA sent two more space probes called *Mariner 6* and *Mariner 7.* These space probes took photos of the Martian surface from a much closer distance.

Mariner 9 is shown here, lifting off and heading for Mars.

All three *Mariner* space probes flew quickly past the planet. They photographed only a small part of Mars. So the mysteries of Schiaparelli's *canali* and life on Mars were not completely solved. *Mariner 9* was the first space probe that actually flew in an **orbit** around Mars. From 1971 to 1972, it took more than 7,000 pictures of almost the entire surface. It was able to focus in on specific features. This helped scientists to study them.

The *Viking* missions

In 1975, NASA sent two **space probes,** *Viking 1* and *Viking 2,* to Mars. In June of 1976, *Viking 1* began to send back photos of the surface of Mars. The pictures were taken by a camera and sent to Earth by way of a radio link. The *Viking* space probes were like the *Mariner* space probes because they used machines, not astronauts, to study Mars. But the *Viking* mission was also very different from the earlier *Mariner* missions.

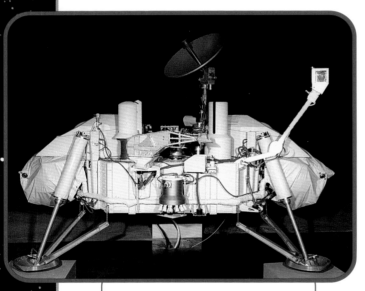

This is a photo of the Viking *lander that was on the surface of Mars.*

Each *Viking* space probe was made of two important parts. The main ship, called the **orbiter,** circled in an **orbit** around Mars. The second part, called the **lander,** was a small spaceship. It had many tools to study the **planet.** Each *Viking* lander left its orbiter when they were close to the Mars **atmosphere.** The lander then went down through the atmosphere of Mars to the surface of the planet.

Viking findings

The *Viking* landers were like small science stations. They had mechanical arms to scoop up rocks and dust from the surface. They also had cameras and small machines to study the surface and atmosphere. They tested the gases in the atmosphere and took many temperature readings. When they finally finished their work in 1982, the *Viking* landers had taken more than 4,500 pictures of Mars.

The *Viking* orbiters were also very busy. Each time they circled the planet, their machines studied many things. They tested the atmosphere, took temperature readings, and recorded the weather patterns. They also took pictures of every part of the planet. By the time the *Viking* mission ended, the orbiters had taken more than 52,000 pictures.

The *Viking lander took many photos of the surface of Mars. Scientists have named the large rock in this photo "Big Joe."*

Where can we land?

Each *Viking* lander was seven feet (two meters) tall and weighed over 1,000 pounds (454 kilograms). Landing on Mars was not an easy job. NASA computers controlled the landers. Controlling a lander is kind of like driving a remote-controlled car. *Viking 1* orbited Mars for more than three weeks before it released its lander. The *Viking 1* lander settled in a rocky area on the surface of Mars. NASA was very lucky when this landing happened, because the *Viking 1* lander did not topple over when it landed on the rocky surface. Another good landing happened later when the *Viking 2* lander reached the ground on the other side of the planet.

The Mars *Pathfinder* mission

On December 4, 1996, NASA sent a **space probe** called *Pathfinder* to Mars. *Pathfinder's* trip was very different from all the other missions to Mars. It cost much less than the other space probes. It weighed much less than the others, too. *Pathfinder* also flew straight to Mars and never **orbited** the **planet** when it arrived. *Pathfinder* used a special protection shield to fly straight into the **atmosphere** of Mars. Then its flight engines were turned off, and *Pathfinder* began to free-fall toward the surface of Mars. When it was five miles (eight kilometers) above the ground, *Pathfinder's* parachutes opened up. This helped to slow down its fall to the surface. Just before *Pathfinder* reached the ground, more than twenty air bags opened up. *Pathfinder* landed on the soft cushion of air bags. It bounced twelve times before it came to rest on the red, dusty soil of Mars.

Pathfinder took wide-range photos like this one to give scientists a better view of the surface of Mars.

Pathfinder was one of the smallest probes that NASA has ever sent to outer space. The **lander** was about the size of a garbage bag. Inside was a small truck called a **rover.** It was about the size of a microwave oven. The rover's job was to travel over the surface, testing the rocks of Mars to see what they are made of. In one

month, the rover traveled only about 20 yards (18 meters). Controlling a rover on Mars is a lot harder than controlling a remote-controlled car. It takes many minutes for a signal to travel from Earth to Mars, so every movement had to be very carefully planned. The *Pathfinder* mission lasted almost three months. During its short time on Mars, *Pathfinder* was able to send back more than 500 photos.

This is the Sojourner *rover that was part of the* Pathfinder *mission to Mars.*

Other missions To Mars

Both the United States and Russia had missions to Mars that did not work. Sometimes the rockets exploded. Sometimes the space probes lost contact when they reached outer space. But every mission to Mars—even the failed missions—has taught us something new and helpful about space exploration. NASA has more missions planned for Mars. Maybe someday soon we will be able to send astronauts to the Red Planet.

How did the *Pathfinder* rover get its name?

NASA asked American schoolchildren to choose the name for the special Mars rover. They named the rover *Sojourner,* after Sojourner Truth. She was a famous African-American woman who fought for the rights of slaves and women in the United States. The word *sojourner* means "explorer."

Fact File

	MARS	EARTH
Average distance from the Sun	142 million miles (228 million kilometers)	93 million miles (150 million kilometers)
Revolution around the Sun	1.9 Earth years	1 Earth year (365 days)
Average speed of orbit	15 miles/second (24 kilometers/second)	18.6 miles/second (30 kilometers/second)
Diameter at equator	7,521 miles (12,104 kilometers)	7,926 miles (12,756 kilometers)
Time for one rotation	24 hours, 37 minutes	24 hours
Atmosphere	carbon dioxide, nitrogen, oxygen, water vapor	oxygen, nitrogen
Moons	2	1
Temperature range	−193°F (−125°C) to 63°F (17°C)	−92°F (−69°C) to 136°F (58°C)

When images of Earth and Mars are placed next to each other, we can see that Earth is much larger.

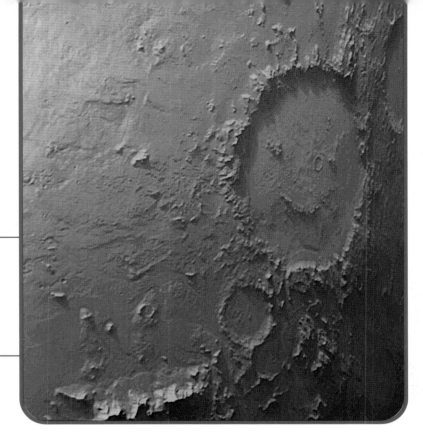

One of the **craters** on Mars looks like a happy face!

A trip to Mars from Earth

- When Mars and Earth come closest to each other in their **orbits,** they are 35 million miles (56 million kilometers) apart.
- Traveling by car at 70 miles (113 kilometers) per hour would take at least 57 years.
- Traveling by rocket at 7 miles (11 kilometers) per second would take at least 58 days.

More interesting facts:

- A person who weighs 75 pounds (34 kilograms) on Earth would weigh about 29 pounds (13 kilograms) on Mars because of the difference in **gravity.**
- There are inactive **volcanoes** on Mars that are larger than the state of Arizona.
- NASA plans to send humans to explore Mars.

Glossary

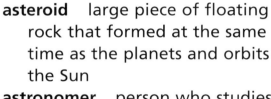

asteroid large piece of floating rock that formed at the same time as the planets and orbits the Sun

astronomer person who studies objects in outer space

atmosphere all of the gases that surround an object in outer space

axis imaginary line through the middle of an object in space, around which it spins as it rotates

chemical reaction when two or more different chemicals mix and cause a physical change

comet ball of ice and rock that orbits around the Sun

core material at the center of a planet

crater bowl-shaped hole in the ground that is made by a meteorite or a burst of lava

crust top layer of a planet that includes the surface

day time it takes for a planet to spin around its axis one time

equator imaginary line around the middle of a planet

gravity invisible force that pulls an object toward the center of another object in outer space

hemisphere one half of a round object in space

lander small spaceship that lands on the surface of a planet or a moon

lava melted rock from inside a planet or moon that pours out onto the surface

magma melted rock inside of a planet or moon

mantle middle layer of a planet or moon. It lies between the core and the crust.

meteor piece of rock or dust that travels in outer space

meteorite piece of rock or dust that lands on the surface of a planet or a moon from space

moon object that floats in an orbit around a planet

opposition opposite position in the sky than the Sun when viewed from Earth

orbit curved path of one object in space moving around another object; or, to take such a path under the influence of gravity

orbiter   spaceship that flies in orbit around a planet

planet   large object in space that orbits a central star, has an atmosphere, and does not produce its own light

revolution   time it takes for a planet to travel one time around the Sun or for a moon to travel around a planet

rover   small truck that is used to study the surface of a planet

solar system   group of objects in space that all float in orbits around a central star

space probe   ship that carries computers and other instruments to study objects in outer space

star   burning ball of gases in outer space that produces light and energy through a process of chemical change

telescope   instrument used by astronomers to study objects in outer space

volcano   mountain built up from layers of hardened lava

year   time it takes for a planet to orbit the Sun one time

More Books to Read

Brimner, Larry Dane. *Mars.* Danbury, Conn.: Children's Press, 1998.

Demuth, Patricia. *Mars: The Red Planet.* New York: Penguin Putnam, 1998.

Kerrod, Robin. *Mars.* Minneapolis, Minn.: Lerner Publications, 2000.

Index